DOUBLE-CROSSED AT CACTUS FLATS

An Up2U Western Adventure

magic
wagon

By: Rich Wallace
Illustrated by: Hazel Mitchell

visit us at www.abdopublishing.com

Printed in the United States of America, North Mankato, Minnesota.
052013
092013
♻ This book contains at least 10% recycled materials.

Written by Rich Wallace
Illustrated by Hazel Mitchell
Edited by Stephanie Hedlund and Megan Gunderson
Cover and interior design by Neil Klinepier

Library of Congress Cataloging-in-Publication Data

Wallace, Rich.
  Double-crossed at Cactus Flats : an Up2U western adventure / by
Rich Wallace ; illustrated by Hazel Mitchell.
      p. cm. -- (Up2U adventures)
  Summary: When young Archer and his partner, Bull, find a silver
vein in the Arizona desert, they think they will be rich, but Cactus
Flats is a town with many dangers and men waiting to double-cross
them, and the reader must choose between three possible endings.
  ISBN 978-1-61641-966-0
  1. Plot-your-own stories. 2. Silver mines and mining--Juvenile
fiction. 3. Western stories. 4. Arizona--Juvenile fiction. [1. Silver
mines and mining--Fiction. 2. Adventure and adventurers--Fiction. 3.
Plot-your-own stories. 4. Arizona--Fiction.] I. Mitchell, Hazel, ill. II.
Title.
  PZ7.W15877Dom 2013
  813.54--dc23
                                                        2013001728

TABLE OF CONTENTS

STRUCK A VEIN

Archer stuck his head out of his bedroll. Something was rustling nearby. The sun wasn't up yet, but there was a bit of light on the horizon.

"Yow!" Archer said. A big, thick snake was coiled a few feet away. The diamondback rattlesnake was shaking its rattles.

Archer scrambled up and grabbed his rifle. The snake uncoiled quickly and slithered away. It was nearly six feet long and as thick as Archer's arm.

Archer watched it go. He easily could have shot it, but they'd be leaving this spot by sunup. So he might as well let the snake get away. It wouldn't bother him again.

"What's the trouble?" asked Bull.

Archer looked at the older man. "There was a big rattler," he said. "It was as long as you are tall."

Bull threw off his blanket and sat up. "That's a good reason to be on our way," he said. He coughed and rubbed his red whiskers. "We can be in Cactus Flats in two hours."

Archer could hear Shadow and Rebel munching on desert grass in the gully below the campsite. The two horses hadn't been spooked by the snake.

"Do we have coffee?" Bull asked.

Archer shook his head. "We drank the last of it yesterday, remember?" he said. "To celebrate."

Bull clapped his hands. "We'll celebrate more tonight," he said. "After we sell some silver."

Bull was a prospector. He roamed the hills and valleys east of Tucson, Arizona, mining for silver and gold. With Archer's help, he'd found a rich vein. Bull had two broken fingers and couldn't dig very well. So, Archer had done a lot of the digging.

Two saddlebags filled with silver ore were hidden back at their claim. Bull had a couple of samples with him. He planned to show them to a mining company in Cactus Flats. For a big reward, he'd lead them to the silver vein.

"I want to be out of here before sunrise," Bull said. "I won't feel safe until I'm in that mining office. There are hundreds of outlaws in this county who would kill us to get that silver."

Archer thought about that. He was pretty sure Bull was an outlaw, too.

Does that make me an outlaw, too? Archer wondered. He hadn't broken any laws. At least none that he knew about. But he'd been riding with Bull for several weeks now. Everything Bull did seemed slightly wrong to Archer. He

wasn't sure that Bull had a right to the silver claim.

But if it wasn't for Bull, where would Archer be? The prospector had kept him safe. In addition to all those outlaws, the Arizona desert was home to unfriendly Apache warriors. Bull knew how to watch for signs of trouble. Archer didn't.

Six months before, Archer had been in school in Oklahoma. But on his fourteenth birthday—January 29, 1882—his father had told him that they were going West. They would join the gold rush and soon be rich.

Now Archer was an orphan. His father had died after a long sickness on the trail. He was buried back in Texas. Archer had made it to Arizona on his own. That's where he met Bull.

Bull also had the idea of striking it rich. And this week, Bull and Archer had found success!

A SHADOW

Archer was hungry. They'd been riding all morning without a bite of food. Finally, they'd reached the top of a hill. They could see the mining town of Cactus Flats about a mile away.

He and Bull stopped their horses. Archer patted Shadow's muzzle. Then he looked over his shoulder. He was sure someone had been following them. That was never a good thing in the desert.

"You're seeing ghosts, boy," Bull said with a laugh. "I'd know in a second if anyone was back there."

Archer took off his tan cowboy hat and ran a hand through his sweaty brown hair. He guessed that the temperature was nearly 100 degrees.

"All morning it has felt as if someone was after us," Archer said. "I haven't seen anyone, but I think someone wants to do us in."

Bull nodded. "Lots of men would want to," he said. "Any prospector would give his right arm to find what we did at our claim. And many of them wouldn't think twice about killing us for it."

Archer looked back again. "Can we eat when we get to town?" he asked.

"Only if you can find a way to eat for free," Bull replied. "I don't have a dollar in my pocket yet, but I've got a million in my heart. This silver will make us rich."

"How can you be sure?" Archer asked. "These hills are studded with gold and silver. Why would the mining company pay you to find it for them?"

Bull reached into his pocket and pulled out a round nugget of silver ore. He held it up between the thumb and a finger of his non-injured hand. Then he closed one eye.

"This is the purest ore I've ever seen," Bull said. "With most ore, you get a $1,000 worth of silver from a ton. Maybe $2,000 if you're lucky."

Bull nodded to Archer. He put the silver nugget back in his pocket, then he smiled. "I'd stake my life that this here ore is worth $15,000 a ton. Maybe more."

That would buy a lot of food. And much, much more.

Archer scanned the desert. The dusty hills had a purple tint. Mesquite bushes and sage plants dotted the landscape. Not far off, the adobe buildings of Cactus Flats shined in the sun.

"That spot was empty just three years ago," Bull said. "Nothing but desert. Nothing! Now there's a hundred buildings, and more being built. All because of the gold and silver."

Archer nodded. He'd never been to Cactus Flats. He hadn't seen a town that big since leaving home.

"A smart man can get very rich out here," Bull said. "But if he's not careful, he can soon be very dead." He laughed. "We're the smart ones. Let's go get rich."

Suddenly Bull stopped smiling. He turned and scanned the hills behind them. Then he spurred his horse and took off.

"Let's go, boy!" he shouted.

Archer spurred Shadow. "What is it?" he called.

"We're not alone after all!" Bull yelled. "Don't you slow down until we reach Cactus Flats!"

NO CREDIT

Archer hopped off his horse outside the Cactus Flats Mining Company. The office was on the street level of one of the few two-story buildings in town. It was between the Golden Eagle Cafe and the sheriff's office.

The street wasn't busy. Most of the men were working in the mines at this hour. And there weren't many women or children in Cactus Flats.

"Do you think someone's onto us?" Archer whispered.

Bull spit a big wad of goo into the dusty street. "Looks like that might be possible," he said. "I finally caught sight of a couple of outlaws back there. It might have been a coincidence that they were nearby. But maybe not."

"Could you identify them?" Archer asked. He wanted to know who they might be up against.

Bull shrugged. "I know one of them. I spent some time with him in Yuma."

"Prospecting?"

Bull let out a snort. "Not quite," he said. "Yuma's a prison."

So Bull had been a prisoner. That didn't surprise Archer. But it didn't make him feel very safe either.

"Were they all bad guys?" he asked.

Bull laughed. "All except me."

They gave their horses water.

Bull placed a hand on Archer's shoulder. "See if you can rustle up some grub for us," he said. "And some coffee." He jutted his head toward the mining company office. "This might take a while."

Archer walked the length of the town and back. Then he went into the café. There were two men at a table eating a late breakfast. One had a thick black mustache and a scar on his cheek. The other was bald and his right eye was mostly closed.

Archer could smell coffee, beans, and meat. He breathed in deeply.

The man behind the counter looked friendly. He was heavy and had long sideburns.

"Any chance for credit?" Archer asked. "I'll be coming into some money very soon."

The man pointed to a sign tacked to the wall: *No Credit*. But he smiled.

"What's your story?" he asked. "Haven't seen you before."

"I just got to town this morning," Archer replied. "Been prospecting."

"Any luck?" the man asked.

Archer gave a tight smile. "Like I said. I'll have some money soon."

The man set a cup on the counter and poured some amber liquid from a white pitcher. "Here's some hot tea," he said. "On the house."

"Much appreciated," Archer said. He sat on a stool and sipped the tea. Even though the day was a scorcher, the hot tea felt good going down.

"I'm Virgil Chandler," the man said. "I own this place. You?"

"Archer Kline." He set down the cup and grinned. "I don't own anything."

"I wouldn't expect you to," Virgil said. "How old are you?"

"Almost fifteen," Archer replied.

"Are you alone?"

"I've been working with a man. We made a claim. Looks like a good one," Archer replied.

Virgil leaned forward. He glanced at the other two customers, but they weren't paying attention. "Gold or silver?"

Archer leaned forward too. He knew he shouldn't say a word about the silver. But Virgil wasn't a prospector. He ran a restaurant.

"Well," Archer said, "suppose you tell me what's for lunch first?"

Virgil smiled. "Antelope stew."

"Sounds mighty good."

"I can't afford to give you credit," Virgil said. "Business hasn't been very good." He raised his eyebrows and tapped his fingers on the counter.

"It's silver," Archer said. "Fifteen miles east of here. It's the richest ore you'll ever see."

It was a huge desert out there. Archer knew that anyone would need a lot more information than that to find the vein.

Virgil stepped into his kitchen. He came back with a big bowl of stew and set it in front of Archer.

"Eat up," he said. "You can pay me some other time. When that money comes in."

Archer thanked him and dug into the stew.

"Silver ore, eh?" Virgil said. He winked. "My advice is do not tell another soul about it. There are a lot of double-crossers in this town."

FiVE GRAND

Archer poured half the stew into a small metal container. He nodded to Virgil, then he went outside to wait for Bull.

He sat on the wooden boards of the sidewalk and leaned against the wall of the mining office. Across the wide dirt street was the Cactus Flats Hotel, the Cochise County Bank, a gambling hall, and a general store.

The door opened and Bull stepped out. He stared straight ahead and walked into the street. He didn't look happy.

Archer followed him. "Wait up!" he called.

Bull slowed a little and Archer caught up. "No luck?" he asked.

"We're still in discussions," Bull said. He scowled as he looked back at the mining office.

"They're thieves, like everybody else in this town. But they know what we've got. They'll wise up."

"What did they say?" Archer asked. "How much is the ore worth?"

Bull let out a scornful laugh. "They said $2,000 a ton. Offered me $5,000 for the claim, if it's real. I told them it's worth twenty times that."

"So now what?" Archer knew a little about how it worked. The mining company would assay, or examine, the ore and decide how much it was worth. Of course they would tell the prospector that it was worth less than it really was. But they'd eventually make a higher offer for really good ore.

"They said someone would ride out there with me this afternoon," Bull said. "Or tomorrow. But they have to put up some cash first. Otherwise we'll find a different company to do business with."

"So, we'll just lay low for now?" Archer asked.

"We'll just lay low," Bull confirmed.

Archer gave Bull the container with the stew. Bull ate it in a hurry. "You should shoot some game for supper," he said. "Get a couple of jackrabbits."

Archer pointed toward the café. "The owner might give us more credit," he said. "I told him we're good for it."

Bull's face turned red. "What did you tell him?" he demanded.

"Nothing." Archer took a step back. "Just that we'd have money soon. He was a nice fella. Name's Virgil."

Bull gripped Archer's shirt in his fist. "Listen to me," he said. "Nobody is 'nice' when it comes to silver and gold."

"He was," Archer repeated. "And I didn't give him any information, I swear. I wouldn't."

"I'll tell you this one time," Bull said. "You start making noise about coming into money and the whole county gets wind of it. It's survival of the fittest out here. Keep your mouth shut. I don't care if it's a café owner or a minister—you can't trust anyone in Cactus Flats!"

"He said the same thing as you did," Archer replied. "That's how I knew I could trust him."

Bull shook his head. "Who else was in there?"

"There were just two cowboys. They weren't paying any attention to me."

"That's what you think," Bull said. "I'll bet they heard every word you said."

"Couldn't have," Archer said. "I was whispering."

"Well, if they didn't hear it from you, they've already heard it from him," Bull said. Then he turned and spit into the street.

Archer looked down at the dirt. He was a good judge of people. Virgil was all right. At least Archer thought he was.

But he wished he had kept his mouth shut.

A NEW GAME

As Bull and Archer were getting their horses, the two cowboys came out of the café. They headed across the street.

Archer watched them go. Then, he climbed into the saddle.

"That bald one was the one from Yuma," Bull said. "They're the ones who were trailing us this morning."

"I didn't say a word to him," Archer said. "Or to the other one."

"They're up to no good," Bull said. "I don't know that one with the mustache. But if he's with Zinger, then he must be as low as they come."

"What do you think they're going to do?" Archer asked.

Bull scowled. "You mean if they don't follow us to the claim? Probably rob the bank."

"Right now?"

"Any time," Bull said. "Zinger is nothing but trouble."

Archer looked at the two outlaws. They were leaning against a rail outside the general store.

Bull pointed toward the café. "You said he gave you some credit?"

"Right. Why?"

Bull hopped off his horse. "I'm mighty parched," he said. "Maybe I can get a drink."

"He gave me some tea," Archer said.

"Maybe he has coffee," Bull replied.

The café was empty now. Virgil was wiping the counter. He waved to Archer and made eye contact with Bull.

"I'd be much obliged if I could have a cup of coffee," Bull said.

Virgil nodded. He poured two cups. Bull and Archer sat down.

"Hot one out there," Bull said.

"Hot in here, too," Virgil replied.

They made small talk for a few minutes about the new buildings being built. Virgil said he'd only been in Cactus Flats for a couple of months.

"Are you doing well?" Bull asked.

Virgil shook his head slowly. "I might have to try a new game."

"Like what?" Bull asked. "Tap dancing?"

"Maybe prospecting." Virgil winked at Archer again. "I heard it can be profitable."

"Yeah, well, it can be mighty hard, too," Bull said. He sounded angry.

Virgil nodded. "You're right. Prospecting is not for me," he said. "I think this café will do just fine. As Cactus Flats grows, we'll get busier."

"That's a fact," Bull said. He held up his injured hand. The first two fingers were stiff and swollen. "Can't hardly do a day's work right now."

"Good thing you have a helper," Virgil said. He glanced at Archer. Archer looked down.

Bull finished his coffee and stood. "He helps," Bull said. He gave Virgil a hard stare. "But sometimes he can't keep his mouth shut."

"He hasn't said a word since you came in here."

29

"He said enough last time," Bull replied. "Didn't he?"

Virgil looked away. "He said very little."

Bull pushed the empty cup toward Virgil. "I hope that's true," he said. "There are too many ears in this town. He needs to learn that if he wants to survive."

STOP THOSE THIEVES!

Archer and Bull headed out of town. They wanted to find a camping spot not far away.

"We'll come back in a couple of hours," Bull said. "Maybe those mining people will have wised up by then."

They hadn't gone far before they heard gunshots.

Within seconds, the two cowboys from the café were racing past on their horses. The bald one fired another shot toward downtown. Then they disappeared behind a hill.

Archer could see a man in a white apron standing in the street outside the general store.

His arm was bleeding and he was yelling, "Stop those thieves!"

"Should we follow them?" Archer asked Bull.

Bull shook his head. "That could take all day. I need to stay around in case the mining company wants to see our claim."

They rode back into town. A small group of men had gathered in the street, including Virgil.

"Where's the sheriff?" Bull asked.

"Gone to Tucson," Virgil replied. "We'll have to get together a posse on our own. Those two robbed the store and shot Carson here in the arm."

"I'll be all right," Carson said. "Someone get the doctor."

Virgil was asking which men would be willing to track down the robbers. "I know exactly where they're headed," he said. "They were in my restaurant just a short while ago. They told me where they're camped."

Someone asked Carson how much money had been stolen.

"Two days worth of sales," Carson said. "A lot of cash."

Bull nudged Archer and pointed toward two men standing outside the mining company. "That's the owner and his assistant," he said.

"Should we talk to them?"

"I just did," Bull replied. "Remember?"

"But we can join the posse if they don't want to see the claim yet," Archer said. "Otherwise we'll need to stay near town."

Bull nodded. "Stay here," he said. He walked quickly to the mining office.

Virgil and four other men were saddling up and getting ready for the chase. "Are you with us?" Virgil called to Archer.

"I'm not sure."

"We need you, boy!" Virgil said. "Let's go."

Bull rushed over. "The assistant said he will ride to the claim with me," he said. "This is a good time to go, with those two outlaws out of the way. You join the posse."

"Why?"

"The farther you chase those outlaws, the better," Bull said.

So Archer jumped onto Shadow and followed Virgil's posse out of town.

Archer was sweating like a mule from the heat and from fear. He urged Shadow forward and they raced after Virgil. With six men on the chase, they'd have plenty of manpower to take down those outlaws.

"Dead or alive!" Virgil called. "We won't look back until those two varmints are out of action!"

RIDING WITH THE POSSE

Archer caught up to Virgil as they passed the hill. "I saw them go that way," Archer said. He pointed beyond the hill to the left.

Virgil shook his head. "They've been camping out by Thunder Ridge," he said. "Even if they went the way you said, they would circle back toward the ridge."

The other riders were 100 yards ahead and moving fast.

"We'll cross the outlaws' path soon," Virgil said. "I know just where they were going."

They did reach some fresh hoofprints in a few minutes, but Archer had no way of knowing whose horses had made them. Virgil seemed to know what he was doing. They turned to follow the tracks.

"Who are those two?" Archer asked.

"Jack Turner has the mustache," Virgil said. "He's a mean one. He's known to have killed six men."

Archer gripped his rifle tighter. He'd never fired it at anything but antelope or rabbits. But today might be different.

"And the bald one?" he asked.

"Zinger Garrett," Virgil replied. "He's a liar and a thief, but he's a better man than Turner."

The rest of the posse was far ahead now. "Should we try to catch up?" Archer asked.

"It's better if we don't all ambush the bandits at once," Virgil said. "I know where they are. We'll sneak up on them."

"How far?" Archer asked.

"Two more miles. Maybe a little more."

They raced past sagebrush and cacti. The desert was hilly, so it was hard to see far ahead.

At last they came over a ridge and saw the rest of the posse stopped just ahead. There were signs of a campfire. Some clothing was scattered on the ground, too. But there were no other signs of the outlaws.

"Looks like they've been here and left," Archer said.

"They wouldn't stay long," Virgil said. He put his hand on his chin and squinted. "We may need to split this posse up. They either headed west or north, I'm certain of that."

As Archer and Virgil rode up, one of the other men hopped off his horse. He started kicking at the ground inside the campfire ring.

"This hasn't been used in a few days," the man said. "You sure this was their camp, Virgil?"

Virgil stepped down, too. "Right here," he said. "They told me that not more than an hour ago."

The man made a sour face and nodded. He turned his head to the right, then to the left.

"There are only two logical ways they could have gone," Virgil said. "It's either west toward Tucson or north into the mountains."

"Tucson makes more sense to me," the man said.

Virgil shook his head. "Not those boys," he said. "They'd want to disappear for a while. I say they went north."

The other man spit and looked up at the sky. "I'm going west." The others nodded and agreed.

"Well, splitting up is a good idea," Virgil said. "I'll take this lad with me."

"How would the two of you handle those outlaws?" the man asked. "You'd both be dead in a minute."

"We'll have to ambush them," Virgil said. "Sneak up and take them when they don't expect it."

That sounded dangerous to Archer. But he didn't like this other man. Virgil seemed much more sensible. He decided to stay with Virgil.

But who ever heard of a two-man posse? Archer gulped and gripped Shadow's reins.

This all sounded like trouble.

DOUBLE-CROSSED

Late in the afternoon, Virgil stopped by a small creek. "We need a rest," he announced.

"Where are we?" Archer asked.

Virgil smiled. "Right where we need to be," he said. "We made the right choice. I know where those outlaws are."

Archer had seen no signs that they were trailing the bandits. Not a hoofprint or anything else could be seen.

"How do you know?" Archer asked.

"You'll see. Now take your gun and get us a jackrabbit. I'll start a fire," Virgil said.

Archer walked a short distance. He was drenched with sweat and was much more thirsty than hungry. But Virgil was a good cook. Some roasted rabbit sounded good.

It didn't take long for Archer to shoot one. He carried it back to the creek and skinned it.

"Go ahead and take a rest," Virgil said. "I'll cook this up and we'll get back on the trail."

"Where did you find wood to burn?" Archer asked.

"I gathered some mesquite roots," Virgil said. "They burn very well."

There was a bit of shade behind some rocks. Archer pulled his hat down low and sat against the rocks. He shut his eyes.

Archer thought about how far he'd come in the past few months. He'd been a boy when he left Oklahoma, but that seemed so long ago. He'd buried his own father after watching him die. That had made Archer grow up in a hurry.

Archer had gone hungry many nights since then. His last shirt was torn and wearing thin. And he had no idea what his future would hold.

43

But then he remembered the silver claim. Bull had said it would make them rich. Suddenly Archer wasn't so sure. He knew it was a great vein of ore. Very valuable.

Bull was probably at that claim right now. He was making a deal with the mining company. Would he include Archer in that deal? Or would he take the money and run? Is that why he sent Archer on the posse?

Bull was a smart prospector. He had a keen sense of where to dig for silver and gold. But with his injuries, he needed someone to do a lot of the labor. Was that all Archer had been good for?

Archer could smell the rabbit cooking. Virgil had rigged up a spit from some branches and was turning it over the coals.

Archer tried to think of better things. But he kept coming back to the silver. Bull wouldn't have needed him if he had two good hands.

Would he decide he didn't need Archer now? Would he double-cross him?

Bull was gruff. He'd been in prison for some reason. But he'd treated Archer well. Archer would just have to hope that he'd continue to do so.

Archer shut his eyes again. That rabbit would take a while longer to cook. He slid a little farther down into the rocks. Virgil was right there, and he was wide awake. He'd keep guard.

Archer yawned and let himself fall asleep. Only a few minutes had gone by when Archer felt a light kick on his boot. He opened his eyes. Virgil was standing there. He had his pistol drawn. He was holding Archer's rifle in his other hand.

"What's wrong?" Archer asked.

Virgil gave a tight smile. "A slight change in plans," he said. "Get on your feet."

"Trouble?" Archer said.

"Not yet."

"Let me have my gun."

Archer heard a click and looked at Virgil's pistol. "Stay right there," Virgil said.

"What's going on?" Archer asked.

"We'll eat," Virgil said, aiming his gun at Archer's chest. "Then you'll take me to that silver claim."

Archer gulped. Bull had been right. He shouldn't have trusted anyone. He had been double-crossed after all.

THEM OR YOU

Archer hadn't eaten much of the rabbit. Whatever hunger he'd had was gone. Virgil was just as bad as anyone. Maybe worse.

They'd been riding toward the silver claim, but it was many miles away. And the sun was going down.

Virgil had both guns. He hadn't said he'd shoot Archer, but the threat was clear. He said that his intent was to ambush Bull and steal all the silver Bull was carrying. But he needed Archer to show him the way to the claim. And those two guns were enough to make Archer do it.

There had been no sign of Bull. Archer hoped he'd made it back to Cactus Flats. Or would Bull and the man from the mining company spend the night at the claim?

"You're certain that this is the route you took?" Virgil asked.

"Dead certain," Archer said. "The claim is straight ahead."

"We'll camp now," Virgil said. "If they're still out there, they couldn't make it back tonight. This is a good place to wait."

Virgil pointed toward a small hill. "We'll wait right there. We'll see them long before they see us."

"There's something you're forgetting," Archer said. "There are two of them. They both have guns. There are two of us, but I'm unarmed."

Virgil squinted. "But I have the advantage. They don't know I'm here."

Archer nodded. "You can only surprise them once," he said. "I think there will be two dead men when this is over. Odds are it'll be one of them and you."

Virgil stared at the hill for a moment. He let out his breath. "So, maybe you and I need to come to an agreement," he said.

"I'm listening."

"Here's the truth," Virgil said. "I don't expect to see your friend Bull coming along this trail. And I don't expect to see the man from the mining company either."

"Then what are we doing here?" Archer asked.

"We're waiting to make an ambush."

"Of who?"

Virgil let out a laugh. "Remember when you said those outlaws had made a left turn going out of town?"

"Yeah. You said they would have circled back toward Thunder Ridge."

Virgil shook his head. "They didn't. I said I knew exactly where they were, remember?

That was the truth. But I didn't say I'd lead the posse to them. I just said I knew where they were."

"So you tricked the posse?"

"I sure did. Those outlaws were laying low until your friend headed for his claim. So I led every available man out of town in the other direction. Those two outlaws waited to follow Bull to his claim. The first big ambush will take place there."

"Is there a second one?" Archer asked.

"There will be," Virgil replied. "Like I said, there will be an ambush right here. And I'll ride away a rich man."

So that was Virgil's plan. He'd made a deal with those outlaws and Archer had been drawn into it. Virgil led the posse in the wrong direction. That gave the outlaws plenty of time to follow Bull.

"Why don't you just let those outlaws do the ambush?" Archer asked. "If you made a deal with them, then they'll owe you a piece of what they steal."

Virgil smiled. "That's what we agreed," he said. "But those two are double-crossers. They'd take that silver and I'd never see them again."

Virgil wiped his chin with his sleeve. "But I'm going to double-cross the double-crossers," he said. "I'll shoot them down and keep that silver for myself."

"But you're outnumbered," Archer said.

"Not if you want in. I'll give you a third of the silver. All you have to do is give me cover. You'll get your gun back. But you have to give me your word that you'll be on my side."

"You already tricked me once," Archer said. "How do I know you won't do it again?"

"What choice do you have?" Virgil said. "I have both guns, remember? You won't survive this shoot-out without one. So you can either take my side or say good night. Forever."

Archer let out his breath. Was Bull already dead? Were those outlaws on their way back right now? Could he overcome Virgil on his own without a gun?

The odds looked bad. Archer stared at Virgil.

Archer and Bull had filled two saddlebags with silver nuggets, and Archer knew where there was more. He could be mighty rich for a teenager if he sold all that silver. Or even a third of it.

If Bull was dead, then why shouldn't Archer get his share? That was better than letting those outlaws have it.

"So, you're telling me I can trust you?" Archer asked.

Virgil patted his holster. "What I'm telling you, kid, is that you don't really have any choice."

A LONG RIDE

Archer didn't sleep at all that night. He sat huddled with his hands around his knees. The desert air turned cold. Virgil said there could be no fire. The smoke would alert those outlaws that someone was nearby.

Virgil slept on the ground, but he kept both guns under his body.

"You'll get your gun when you need it," he said as the sun went down. "I'll keep it right here until then."

Archer knew that Virgil didn't trust him. He shouldn't. If Archer had his gun right now he'd use it. But tomorrow, when those outlaws approached, he'd have to side with Virgil. That was his only chance. The outlaws would kill them both if they could.

So Archer shivered. He hoped he'd make it out of this alive. If things turned out right, he'd be on his way to Tucson tomorrow with some silver nuggets.

If things turned out wrong, he'd be nothing but a meal for some vultures. Or coyotes. He could hear them howling in the distance.

Was Bull dead? If the plan had worked, the outlaws had surely shot him down. Or maybe they'd just tied him up.

The moon rose in the middle of the night, brightening the sky. The world was so vast out here in the desert. Despite his fear, Archer couldn't help but notice how beautiful it was.

Virgil woke with the first hint of daylight.

"They'll be here soon," he said. "Are you with me?"

Archer scowled, but he nodded. "Like you said, I have no choice."

"Check the horses," Virgil said.

Archer walked halfway down the hill. Shadow was grazing on some sparse growth. Archer looked up. Could he get away? Would Virgil shoot him in the back if he climbed up on Shadow to escape?

Archer patted Shadow's side. How far could he get? He had no gun. No food. Very little water. Could he make it back to Cactus Flats alone?

"You wouldn't get fifty feet!" Virgil called. "Don't even think about it, boy."

Archer just stared at Virgil. This wasn't the right time to escape. But maybe when those outlaws were in sight? Virgil would have to give him his gun. And Virgil would be shooting at the outlaws, not him.

"Bring those horses up here!" Virgil said. "Saddle them up, too."

Archer did as he was told. It wouldn't be long now. He sat on a rock near Virgil and waited.

He saw two men on horseback in the distance.

"You ready?" Virgil asked.

"Yep."

"It's too late to shoot me now," Virgil said. "They'd hear the gunshot. Believe me, they'd be on you in a second."

"Why would they do that?"

"You're forgetting one important thing," Virgil said. "They still think I'm on their side." He handed Archer the rifle. "I'm their friend. Remember that. Now get ready to shoot them dead."

THE ENDING IS UP2U!

If you think Archer joins with Virgil and tries to ambush the outlaws, continue reading on page 60.

If you think Archer tries to overcome Virgil and see if he can rescue Bull, turn to page 67.

If you think Archer should jump on Shadow and try to escape, turn to page 74.

ENDING 1: A SECOND CHANCE

The outlaws were approaching quickly. Archer could see the dust rising up behind the horses as they ran.

Archer wiped a sweaty hand on his shirt, then took aim. If those men had killed Bull, then Archer wanted revenge. And he also wanted to stay alive!

But he was going to let Virgil fire first.

"I want your word that you'll share the silver with me," Archer whispered.

Virgil nodded. "You have it," he said. "Do I have yours?"

"Yes."

"Then let's get this done," Virgil said. "We'll be rich in a minute if this goes right."

Virgil fired his gun. Zinger Garrett fell from his horse and hit the ground. He rolled over and yelled. Then he lay still in the dirt.

A return shot from Jack Turner hit Virgil. He stumbled backward, bleeding from his chest. Archer jumped to his side.

"Are you all right?" Archer said.

But before Virgil could reply, Archer felt a red-hot pain in his arm. He dropped to his knees and grabbed his arm with his other hand.

Archer's hand came away bloody. His arm felt as if someone had dug a knife into it. He'd been shot. Would another bullet soon be on its way?

Archer dropped flat. The burning pain was intense. Over the hill he could see Jack

Turner standing by Zinger's horse. Zinger lay motionless in the dirt.

Should Archer shoot? The pain was so bad that he didn't know if he could aim. And if he missed, Turner would certainly shoot him.

Archer reached for his gun. He'd dropped it when the bullet hit. Then he watched as Turner grabbed a saddlebag from Zinger's horse. He leaped back onto his own horse and galloped away.

Archer gave a sigh of relief. He felt his arm again. The pain was severe, but he'd only been nicked. There didn't seem to be a bullet in his arm. If he could get back to Cactus Flats, the doctor could take care of it.

Virgil moaned. Archer looked down and saw the blood spreading through his shirt. The ground around him had already turned red. Within seconds, Virgil was dead.

Archer sat still for several minutes. He was sweaty and shaking.

The horses had run off, but Archer called for Shadow. He peeled Virgil's pistol from the dead man's hand, then stood up. Shadow had trotted to the bottom of the hill. Archer walked down.

"You need to get me to safety," Archer said. He was dizzy and scared. He scanned the horizon, looking for Turner, but all he could see was a trail of hoofprints headed north.

Turner had all the silver. He wouldn't be coming back.

It was hard, but Archer managed to get into the saddle. He coaxed Shadow to move. The pain was worse than anything Archer had ever felt, but at least he was alive. Two men were lying dead in front of him. And Bull and the man from the mining company must be dead, too.

Archer gritted his teeth and turned Shadow toward Cactus Flats. The burning was getting worse. Every movement sent pain through his arm. He gripped the saddle horn with his other hand.

"Just get me back," Archer whispered.

Shadow began to run faster, but the bumping caused too much pain in Archer's arm. He pulled back on the reins to get the horse to slow down.

Archer kept looking around to make sure Turner wasn't coming back. He could fire a gun if he had to, but Archer was so dizzy that he couldn't see straight. He'd be no match for that outlaw.

A movement in the dirt caught Archer's eye. It was a rattlesnake, as big as the one he'd seen the day before. Shadow stepped quickly away from it. Archer just stared.

This desert was full of snakes. But Archer had let one survive yesterday when he could have shot it. Now he had a second chance, too. Instead of being shot dead in the desert, he could make a better life for himself.

After what seemed like the longest ride of his life, Archer could finally see Cactus Flats in the distance. He let out a sigh of relief. He would survive this and move on to something better.

ENDING 2: DON'T THINK TOO HARD

Virgil had double-crossed him. How could Archer trust him now? He gripped the rifle.

Virgil was focused on the two outlaws. Within a minute they'd be in shooting range. The dust was rising high behind the running horses.

Archer took aim. Those men had probably killed Bull. He wanted revenge. But he also wanted to live.

Archer glanced sideways at Virgil. He could turn his gun and shoot him dead now. Maybe the outlaws would just keep going. Maybe he could escape. He began to turn the gun.

Virgil reached out and gripped the gun's barrel. He held it steady and stared at Archer.

"Pull the trigger," Virgil said. "I dare you!"

Archer just stared back.

"Pull it!" Virgil said.

Archer pulled the trigger. There was nothing but a click.

"I figured you'd try something like that," Virgil said. "That's why that gun is empty." He reached into his holster for some ammunition. "Load up or we'll both be dead men!"

But there was no time to load. The riders were nearly upon them. Virgil fired his gun, and Jack Turner flew off his horse. He hit the dirt and came to a dead stop.

Zinger Garrett stood in his stirrups and shot back. The blast hit Virgil square in the chest. Virgil fell backward and blood spurted from a huge wound.

69

Archer dove to the dirt and lay face down. Zinger kept riding. In a minute, he was just a cloud of dust on the horizon.

Virgil and Turner were lying motionless in pools of blood. The horses had run off, but Archer called for Shadow.

Would Zinger be coming back? Not if he had all the silver. But Archer didn't plan to wait around. Two dead men were enough. He didn't want to be the third.

And what about Bull and the man from the mining company? Were they dead, too? Archer couldn't leave without finding out.

Shadow had trotted to the bottom of the hill. Archer climbed into the saddle and rode.

Within a mile he saw two horses tethered to a low tree. One of them was Bull's horse, Rebel.

Then he saw a dead man lying sprawled out in the dirt. It was the man from the mining company.

Archer rode past.

Bull's silver claim was inside a cave at the side of a rocky hill. Archer stopped outside the entrance and shouted.

"Bull?"

A few seconds passed. Then a hoarse voice said, "Archer?"

Archer felt tears of joy. He jumped from the horse and climbed into the narrow hole. Bull was tied up, but he was alive.

"Why didn't they kill you?" Archer asked.

"I don't know," Bull said. "After I gave them the saddlebags, I figured they'd shoot me dead. But I told them there was more silver hidden nearby. I said I'd show them if they'd promise to let me live."

"And they agreed?"

"They did," Bull said. "I was sure they'd kill me anyway. But Zinger said he'd never kill a fellow prison mate if he didn't have to. So they tied me up. They probably figured I'd starve to death anyway."

Archer felt dizzy. He'd been through so much. Had any of it been worth it?

Bull pulled out a handful of silver pebbles. "There's still a lot of silver in this claim," he said. "We might wind up rich after all."

"But this is such dangerous country," Archer said. "The mining company already lost a man out here. Do you really think they'd want to pay you for this claim?"

"It's great ore," Bull replied. "Worth the risk."

Archer wasn't sure about that. He'd seen more risks in the past twenty-four hours than he'd like to see in a lifetime. He'd seen two men shot to death this morning. Another was lying dead not fifty yards away.

"Let's get back to Cactus Flats," Archer said. "I have a lot of thinking to do."

"Don't think too hard," Bull said with a grin.

Archer didn't grin back. Couldn't a man make an honest living out here without risking his life? Maybe not in Cactus Flats. Perhaps he should move along to California.

He knew two things for certain. This adventure had nearly cost him his life. And his life was worth much more than silver.

ENDING 3: THE END OF THE LINE

"This rifle's empty!" Archer yelled. "Why did you unload it?"

"Because I thought you'd try to shoot me," Virgil answered.

"My ammunition is in my saddle bag," Archer said. He walked swiftly down the hill toward Shadow.

"Get back here!" Virgil yelled.

"I'm no good without ammo!" Archer hollered back.

Archer ducked when he heard Virgil fire his gun. But Virgil had fired at the outlaws, not him. This was his chance to escape!

Archer climbed into the saddle and spurred Shadow. Which way should he go?

Archer kept low in case Virgil tried to shoot him. But the gunfight was blaring, with Virgil and the two outlaws shooting at each other. Virgil had no time to think about Archer.

Archer circled the hill on Shadow. He couldn't see the others, but he heard more gunfire. Virgil yelled out in pain. He'd been shot.

Shadow raced toward the side of the hill. If Archer chose wrong, he'd be face-to-face with the outlaws. If he chose right, they'd never know he was there. He could keep riding into the hills. He'd be free of those people forever.

Archer froze when he heard hoofbeats behind him. He swung around in his saddle and raised his rifle. But it was just Virgil's horse trailing them. He was scared, too.

A hundred yards away, Jack Turner raced by on his horse. Then he turned north. Within seconds, Turner and his horse were nothing but a cloud of dust in the distance.

But what about Zinger Garrett? Archer tugged on the reins to stop Shadow. Then he inched forward again.

As they rounded the hill, they came face-to-face with Zinger's horse. But the horse was without a rider. Zinger lay flat on his face nearby. The ground around him was red with blood.

Archer knew that Virgil had been shot, too. But was he dead? Or was he stalking Archer now, ready to shoot him down?

Keeping his rifle up and ready to shoot, Archer inched up the slope. And there was Virgil, lying in a pool of blood. Archer nudged him with his rifle. He was dead.

Would Turner be coming back? Not if he had all the silver. But Archer didn't plan to wait around. Two dead men were enough. He didn't want to be the third.

The sun was up now, and the heat was already setting in. Archer headed toward Bull's claim.

Soon he saw Bull's horse, Rebel, tethered to a tree. Not far away, Bull and the man from the mining company were sprawled out in the dirt. They were dead, too. Shot by those outlaws.

The claim was inside a cave at the side of a rocky hill. Archer stopped outside the entrance. The two saddlebags were gone, but Archer knew where there was more silver.

It wasn't much, but he pulled a small bag of nuggets from a hole in the wall. Then he rode back to Bull.

"You were a good man," Archer said as he stood over Bull's body. "It turns out you were the only one I could trust. I'll never forget it."

Archer unhooked Bull's canteen and took a long drink of water. Then, Archer clipped the canteen onto his own belt. "Thanks again," he said.

He took the mining man's canteen, too. Without water, Archer would have no chance to cross the desert. He had a long ride ahead of him. He wasn't sure where he was headed, but he wanted no part of this desert any longer.

Archer and Shadow ran as fast as they could, back the way they came. Archer never wanted to see this silver claim again. And Cactus Flats held no appeal, either.

"I hope you can make it to Tucson," he said to Shadow. "It's time for a new start on life."

But Archer knew Tucson wouldn't be the end of the line for him. He'd learned a lot in the past few months. He knew one thing for certain. Being alive was better than dying in the desert.

WRITE YOUR OWN ENDING

There were three endings to choose from in *Double-Crossed in Cactus Flats*. Did you find the ending you wanted from the story? Did you want something different to happen?

Now it is your turn! Write an ending you would like to happen for Archer, Bull, Virgil, and the outlaws. Be creative!